Witch-in-
Training

Task

Other Witch-in-Training titles

Witch-in-Training
The Last Task

Maeve Friel

Illustrated by Nathan Reed

HarperCollins *Children's Books*

First published in Great Britain by HarperCollins *Children's Books* 2005
HarperCollins *Children's Books* is a division of HarperCollins *Publishers* Ltd
77-85 Fulham Palace Road, Hammersmith, London W6 8JB

The HarperCollins *Children's Books* website address is
www.harpercollinschildrensbooks.co.uk

Text © Maeve Friel 2006
Illustrations © Nathan Reed 2006

ISBN 978-0-00-718527-6

Chapter One

Jessica had had a busy year training to be a witch with Miss Strega. It goes without saying that she was a *modern* witch; she did *not* have a greasy old cape and a hooked nose, she did *not* conjure up nasty smelling brews (except sometimes, for a laugh) and she *always* flew her broom the Right-Way-Up – with the twigs in front.

"The best thing about being a witch," Jessica was thinking as she zipped over the rooftops, "is all the *stuff* you get. As well as my broom and my helmet and my flying licence, I have my lucky pebble, my wand, my long-eared owl's feather for mingling brews..."

"Hu-eet," whistled Berkeley indignantly, poking her head out of Jessica's cape pocket.

"And you, especially, my wonderful mascot. I was just about to say that."

She stroked the nightingale's feathery neck and then, as Miss Strega's chimney pots came into view, flicked the descend twig of her broom, swooped down and made a perfect landing on the roof of the hardware shop.

"The *other* best thing about being a witch," she told Berkeley, "is knowing Miss Strega. Not that she doesn't make me do some very hard things, like switching myself into a cat or vaulting over the moon. I wonder what I will have to do next."

She was just about to clamber through the attic window when she heard voices in the shop below.

"That's odd. Miss Strega's customers don't usually come until later."

She glided over to the attic trapdoor which was directly above the shop counter, opened it just a smidgen and peered down.

Miss Strega had a visitor.

All that Jessica could see at first was the hem of the visitor's cape and a pair of very high shoes, with heels as slender as needles.

"Oh!" gasped Jessica. She had once met someone who wore shoes like that.

She opened the trapdoor a little more.

Now she could see a tartan triangle of scarf draped over the shoulders of a smart glossy cape.

"Tartan? Could it be...?"

She opened the trapdoor a little more.

The visitor was wearing a floppy black velvet hat secured with a long wand-shaped hatpin with a silver thistle at the tip. Even though she could not see her face, there was no doubt who she was.

"Heckitty Darling!" Jessica shouted. "You're back."

She flung the trapdoor wide open and whooshed down into the shop.

Heckitty Darling – for it was indeed the glamorous Scottish actress witch who had

presented Jessica with her flying licence –
turned, theatrically threw her cape over her
shoulder and held out her arms.

"Jessica sweetikins!" she boomed, as if
she were on a stage in front of hundreds of
people, and not in a tiny little shop on the
High Street. "You're looking divine!"

Then she lowered her voice and whispered confidentially. "I was just telling Miss Strega that there has been a break-in at our Coven Garden headquarters. The Witches World Wide guild is up in arms. Our greatest treasure is," Heckitty's voice wobbled, "gone!"

Felicity, Miss Strega's ginger cat, who was snoozing in her usual place on a pile of Spell Books on the counter, opened one orange eye and gave Jessica a wink.

"Our greatest treasure stolen?" said Jessica, looking from Felicity to Heckitty to Miss Strega and back again. "But what is our greatest treasure?"

Miss Strega hopped off her stool and picked up a large ladle. "Why don't I pour us all a nice stiff brew first and then Heckitty can begin at the beginning?"

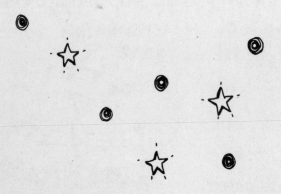

Chapter Two

"Have you ever heard," Heckitty began, when they had all sat down with their cups of joobious juice, "of the Feet First Fund?"

Jessica shook her head.

"No? Well, it's an organisation that finds

and preserves shoes that have made history or that belonged to important people. It was set up by the Literary and Historical Association of the Witches World Wide guild. I am the Head Finder and Seeker."

Jessica and Miss Strega exchanged a look. The look meant *Heckitty Darling is off her rocker*, but Heckitty didn't notice. She carried on.

"You have heard of the old lady who lived in the shoe (she had so many children she didn't know what to do)? Well, we have that shoe. It was our first acquisition. We have one of Cinderella's glass slippers. We have Puss in Boots' boots and Pinocchio's clogs; we have the bootees that belonged to the Wicked Witch of the West... "

Miss Strega replaced her cup on her saucer very noisily. "Yes, yes, my dear Heckitty. We get the idea – but has this got anything to do with the burglary?"

Heckitty looked miffed. Like all actresses, she was a bit of a show-off and expected everyone to listen to her all the time. She sighed.

"Go on," said Jessica. "I think the Feet First Fund sounds brilliant."

Heckitty Darling smiled prettily and moved her stool closer to Jessica's.

"The treasure, the *absolute* pearl of our collection, is a pair of shoes that had once belonged to that wonderful witch, the inventor of the Modern Witch's Right-Way-Up broom, dear Dame Walpurga of the Blessed Warts.

I discovered them at the bottom of Walpurga's well myself, you know, despite what Professor Cobbleroni says."

"Who's Professor Cobbleroni?" asked Jessica.

"Oh, she runs that ridiculous Fancy Footwear Foundation. Anyway, I had hardly put the Dame's shoes on display when they disappeared! I turned my back and *puff!* – they were gone."

"But who took them?" asked Jessica.

Heckitty Darling raised her shoulders and let them drop. "We've no idea. We had had a lot of witch school tours that day so at first I suspected a prank. I tried any number of anti-vanishing spells to make the shoes reappear, but nothing worked. Then we organised a witch hunt. Oodles of witches took part, but the Dame's shoes were nowhere to be found."

Heckitty Darling's voice trembled again. "I'm afraid they may be gone for good."

"Goodness gracious," said Jessica.

"Fortunately," said Heckitty, dabbing at her nose with a handkerchief, "I had the excellent idea of consulting an oracle."

"I once had to consult an oracle myself," said Jessica, proudly. "It was a talking sea anemone on one of the Charm Islands."

Heckitty looked affronted. She obviously had not expected Jessica to know anything about oracles.

"A talking sea anemone? How preposterous! The oracle that I went to is a Greek witch. She's easily the best fortune teller in the world – people *flock* to ask her questions. Unfortunately, she tends to answer in riddles; it can be simply *impossible* to understand a word she says."

Behind her, Miss Strega's cup rattled once again.

"So, the long and the short of it," Heckitty continued, "is that last night when the curtain came down on the show in Coven Garden, (have you seen my reviews, darlings? Simply marvellous!) I flew to the oracle to ask where the shoes could be. This is what she said…"

Heckitty closed her eyes and began to speak in a very strange unearthly voice.

"To find the shoes, no witch is fit
But she who is not a witch as yet
Must fly to where a giant stands.
The answer lies beneath his hands. "

She opened her eyes and spoke in her normal voice.

"What do you make of that?"

"Weird," said Jessica.

"Absolutely baffling," agreed Miss Strega.

"Unless," said Jessica, holding up a finger, "I have a hunch.

Perhaps the oracle is saying that only a witch-in-training can find the shoes – *she who is not a witch as yet.*"

Heckitty clapped her hands together. "By the hooting of Minerva's owl, Miss Strega, I think Jessica's got it."

"Bravo, my little lamb's lettuce!" agreed Miss Strega.

Heckitty Darling opened her handbag and, with a flourish, thrust an envelope into Jessica's hands.

"So, will you take on the Feet First Fund challenge? Will you track down Dame Walpurga's missing shoes?"

Jessica's jaw dropped.

"But, but," she stammered. "Where should I... how do I... what'll... when..."

"Jessica," said Miss Strega sternly. "You're gibbering. I think it's a splendid idea. There's nothing more exciting than a quest. Of course you must do it."

Chapter Three

When Heckitty had left to tell the Feet First Fund
how Jessica had agreed to help find the shoes,
Jessica opened the envelope. It contained a
colour photograph of Dame Walpurga's shoes
on display in the Shoe Salon at Coven Garden.

They were purple boots with pearly buttons up the side and a tassel at the top and might once have been quite pretty, but they were in a terrible condition. The heels were stumpy and lopsided, the toes were scuffed and scratched, and the tassels had seen better days.

Jessica shook her head. "I don't believe it! These shoes may have been Walpurga's but they're wrecked. Whoever took them must be her Number One Fan, because nobody else would wear them."

Miss Strega tapped her nose. "Possibly not, but look at the label.

The Dress Shoes Worn by Dame Walpurga of the Blessed Warts at the Signing of the Treaty to End the Broomstick Battles."

"The Broomstick Battles?" said Jessica. "I did a project about that. Dame Walpurga led the modern witches (who flew with the twigs in front) against the cross old-fashioned witches (who flew with the twigs at the back). It was your grandmother Pluribella who led that bunch..."

Miss Strega blushed. She didn't like to be reminded about how her granny flew the Wrong-Way-Up.

"Never mind about that. The point is, not only are these shoes *antique*, they are *historic*. They are *relic*s of one of the most important witches ever and that means they are *invaluable*."

"In that case," said Jessica, "I'd better take on the quest and do my bit for Witches World Wide."

Miss Strega clapped her hands. "That's my girl. Now, do you still wear those magic pins for getting yourself out of trouble, the ones that Pelagia gave you when you learned Charming? You'll need all the help you can get on a quest."

"Oh yes," said Jessica, touching the row of pins on her cape. "I even have some I've never used before, like this Lantern Fish pin that glows in the dark."

"Good. And be sure to switch on your

super-duper de-luxe invisibility-when-you-need-it cape at the slightest sign of trouble."

"Of course," agreed Jessica. "I'm just wondering where to start my quest. Where would you begin?"

"I'd say, first find your giant."

"But I haven't the foggiest idea where giants live."

"Moonrays and marrowbones, Jessica! Haven't I told you before that you'll never know what you'll find until you start looking? Just hop on your broom and take to the air. Fingers and toes crossed a giant will appear. I'll come with you for the ride."

So off they flew, up into the twinkly night sky, over the rooftops of the High Street and on and on beyond the town and over the river.

At last they saw a tall craggy mountain
that reared up blackly in front of them with
a row of jagged peaks like a rusty worn-
down saw. The air began to throb with a
strange whirring and humming which grew
louder and louder as they flew up over the
peaks. And there on the far side of the
mountain, they discovered the reason for the

eerie humming – a tall spindly windmill with a red conical roof and a pair of over-sized sails rotating furiously in the wind.

They immediately tweaked their Fast Descend twigs and cruised down to have a look but they had not gone very far when the moving air all around them began to whisper and hiss.

"By the swivelling of my arms, something witchy this way comes."

Jessica stopped in mid-air. "Golly, Miss Strega, did you hear that?"

"Pssssssssstttttt," whispered the mill. "Come and sssshake handsssss."

Jessica looked doubtful. Just one touch from one of those great spinning arms and she would surely be hurled to the very farthest corner of the Milky Way. But the wind at that moment began to die away and the mill slowed to a creaking halt. As it did so, a remarkable thing happened.

The windmill began to change.

Its stilts became long lanky legs planted in the heather. Its sails turned into long skinny arms which hung down stiffly at its sides. A knobbly scarred face scowled insolently at them under a red conical hat.

"By the blustery breezes of Old Castile!" Miss Strega gasped. "It looks like this windmill is actually..."

"...a giant!" Jessica exclaimed.

"You with the silly plaits!" the giant wheezed. "Come over here."

"What did you say?" said Jessica.

"I said come over here. I haven't got all day."

"There's no call to be so rude," Jessica retorted.

"Oh, go on," Miss Strega interrupted.

"Go and see what he wants. You needed to find a giant anyway, rude or not. I'll wait here for you."

Jessica edged forward until she was hovering about two broom lengths from the giant's arms. "I'm on a quest," she began, shouting to be heard above his creaking and groaning. "Can you tell me what lies beneath your arms?"

"Speak up!" the giant ordered. "I can't hear you properly."

Jessica nudged her broomstick a little closer.

Suddenly the giant lurched forward and snatched her hand.

"Wey-hey!" he roared.

He carried her up, up and away, spinning her around until her eyes were popping.

"Miss Strega!" she yelled. "He's switched into a windmill again! Stop! Whoa! I'm going to be sick!"

But the giant paid no attention.

Now, just imagine how it feels when you are rotated three hundred and sixty degrees at top speed at the outer end of a windmill's sail. Or should that be at the end of a giant's arms? No wonder Jessica found it hard to think straight. No wonder she felt hard done by as the sails first plunged headlong towards the heathery bog below her and then lurched skywards.

"I am definitely going to be sick," she shrieked.

"Hu-eet," whistled Berkeley cheerfully, bustling out of her pocket to keep her spirits up.

Chapter Four

Luckily, all those months of witch training had not been wasted on Jessica. Even as she was whizzing around like a Catherine Wheel she remembered that she had tricks of her own up her sleeve.

"I have skills," she reminded herself. "No cheeky giant or runaway windmill (or whatever this is) can treat me like this and get away with it. Besides, I must get on with my quest."

So, in mid-hurtle, she composed an incantation and yelled it at the top of her voice into the wind.

"O, Hazel Wand and White Owl's Feather,
Lucky Pebble, Charming Pins,
Draw your magic all together,
Stop this giant; halt these spins!"

The very next moment, she went flying off into space like a cork shooting out of a bottle and landed with a thump on a mossy clump of heather. A moment later, there was an ear-piercing scream and a loud crash which made the whole mountain shudder.

"Aaayyyy caarrrrrammbaaaa!"

When the stars stopped spinning and the earth stopped juddering, Jessica crawled on to her knees and stood up. The giant was sitting some way off, gingerly patting his head and examining his legs for broken bones. "That was a bit rough, wasn't it? A bit uncalled for?"

He cracked his fingers and thumbs loudly.

"What sort of witch are you anyway?"

"I'm a witch-in-training actually," Jessica replied, indignantly.

"I knew there was something funny about you. I said to myself, *Don Gigantesco, she's not up to the job. She's too young,* I said. *Not bright enough.*"

"What job? Do you mean finding Dame Walpurga's shoes?"

"Shoes? What are you blathering about, you daft girl? I mean, not bright enough to turn me back into a giant. Not up to the job of undoing the spell that Pengelly put on me. I've been turning into a windmill every time the wind got up, every day, all day, for the last week – ever since he imprisoned me here on this crag, with my feet stuck in this sopping bog." He flexed his arms and groaned. "It's not been much fun, I can tell you. *And* you certainly took your time getting here."

Jessica narrowed her eyes. "Of all the rude ungrateful giants! I didn't have anything to do with turning you into a windmill. So why did you snatch me?"

The giant stretched his neck and swivelled it around. "What else could I do? I've never been any good at spelling so I needed a witch to come along and undo Pengelly's curse. Mind you, there was no call to send me flying like that. If I have whiplash, you'll be hearing from my solicitors." He cracked his knuckles, stood up and stamped his feet, scattering Jessica's socks, scarf and cape with flecks of mucky water.

Jessica was sorely tempted to turn Don Gigantesco back into a windmill, but she needed information. "Who did you say turned you into a windmill?"

"Pengelly, that blinking gnome. He has a nasty habit of kidnapping giants to run his machinery. No manners. None."

The giant pulled off a sock, squeezed the bog water out of it and shook it in Jessica's direction.

"Does he live around here, this Mr Pengelly?" asked Jessica, wiping her face.

The giant jabbed an arm at the ground. "Do they teach you witches nothing at school these days? Why, the caverns down there are *riddled* with gnomes, hammering and banging night and day."

"Oh," said Jessica and hurriedly climbed aboard her broomstick.

"Hey!" shouted the giant as Jessica took off. "Before you go, could you help me find my seven league boots? They must've sunk into the bog while I've been rotating."

"No!" said Jessica, very sharply. "I must fly!"

She shot off to rejoin Miss Strega and Felicity who were waiting for her on the summit.

They set up camp as soon as the giant set off down the mountain. The earth quaked with every thudding step he took. Jessica

kept watch to make sure he didn't come back while Miss Strega prepared the cauldron of muncheon, their midnight snack.

The marvellous thing about witch's muncheon is that it tastes of whatever you like, so out of the same pot Jessica was having pizza Hawaii, while Miss Strega was looking forward to crab cakes with a

sweet chilli sauce.

"Great spelling, poppet," said Miss Strega, when Jessica explained what had happened with Don Gigantesco. "You must write that one down for future reference, in case you are ever hijacked by a windmill-cum-giant again. Now do tell me, how is your quest coming along?"

Jessica picked a bit of pineapple off her pizza and put it in her pocket for Berkeley. "Well," she said, "the giant was a horrible bad-mannered brute and he didn't know a thing about Dame Walpurga's shoes – but he did say that there is a gnome called Pengelly in a cavern underneath this mountain so I think that must be 'the answer that lies beneath his hands'. Now I must find the entrance to the cavern and interview Pengelly."

"Very wise," Miss Strega began. "I think that..."

But before she had time to tell Jessica what she was thinking, an ominous rumbling started up somewhere deep beneath them. Wispy funnels of steam began to seep through the grass. The muncheon cauldron swayed wildly, tumbled off its stand and

disappeared down a crack that had suddenly appeared in the ground.

"Mmeoowww!" yowled Felicity.

"Moonrays and Marrowbones!" shouted Miss Strega.

"Hu-eeeeet!" shrilled Berkeley.

"All aboard," yelled Jessica, springing to her feet and reaching for her broomstick.

"Crikey! Help!"

With an ear-splitting wrench, the ground beneath her feet splintered and split open and Jessica went tumbling into the gaping hole.

Chapter Five

When Jessica came to, she found herself lying on her back, staring up at a patch of sky and the hole she had fallen through.

She was in a cave dimly-lit by the light of the half-moon. Rocks like immense organ pipes hung down from the roof, gleaming gold where the moonlight struck them. An entire garden of solid stony trees, flowers and giant mushrooms grew out of the floor. There was a musical plip-plop of dripping water.

From way back in the dark tunnel came the sound of scraping.

Rats? Jessica wondered. She shivered and got shakily to her feet. She picked up her broomstick and looked around. Miss Strega and Felicity were nowhere to be seen, but Berkeley was sitting on the ground looking a bit dazed. She fluttered over and sat on Jessica's shoulder.

They began to pick their way around the rocks, stumbling on the uneven ground, feeling the walls, looking for a way out, but the further Jessica moved from the circle of moonlight, the harder it was to see where she was going.

"Miss Strega?" she called into the darkness, but no answer came.

"What I need is a torch," she thought. And no sooner had she said it than she remembered that she *did* have a torch – the magic Lantern Fish pin that her Charm teacher, Pelagia, had given her. As soon as she popped it on the end of her wand, it glowed so brightly it lit up the whole cave. Holding the wand out in front of her, she was able to stoop beneath the rocks without banging her head and skirt around the stone pillars that looked like bearded wizards.

As she walked deeper into the cave, she found the steps of a staircase cut into the rocks. A large notice was nailed to the wall:

Hard Hat Area
Protective footwear
MUST be worn!

The sound of scraping grew louder and closer. The air grew hotter. Clouds of steam billowed up the stairs.

"Brilliant!" said a gruff voice. "That's all I need. The giant must be on the blink again. And that means Muggins here will have to go up and reset him."

Jessica tiptoed further down the steps.

At the bottom, there was a short round bearded manikin leaning on a spade in front of a conveyor belt heaped with piles of glittering rocks. He was wiping the sweat from his neck and face with a large spotted handkerchief.

"Bother and double bother!" he grumbled.

Jessica coughed. "Mr Pengelly?"

The gnome, startled, wheeled around. He held up his spade to shade his eyes from the luminous glow of the Lantern Fish.

"Turn off that light!" he snarled. "I can't be doing with bright lights in my cavern. Don't you know I'm a gnome! Where did you come from anyway?"

"I fell though the roof," said Jessica, shielding the Lantern Fish with one hand. "There was a sort of earthquake and..."

"Earthquake, my foot! My bellows exploded, more like. And now the conveyor belt's conked out. Kaput. Broken. I daresay that good-for-nothing giant is slacking off. He's supposed to keep this machinery moving."

"If you mean Don Gigantesco," Jessica interrupted, "well, he's gone. I made up a spell and..."

"...and let him go?" Pengelly screamed. "You young witches, you come in here, spelling mad, freeing my giants, making my mountain blow up, bringing in lights!"

Jessica wriggled her nose. "I'm just trying to find a missing pair of shoes."

Pengelly looked shifty. He squinted at her and blew his nose vigorously with his spotted handkerchief.

"Shoes?" he asked, nervously scraping the dirt off one of his steel-capped boots with the heel of the other one. "What sort of shoes?"

"A pair of historic witch's shoes. They've been stolen."

"You won't find any witch's shoes down here. Now scram. Hop it." He plunged his spade deep into the lumps of gold and began shovelling them up on to the conveyor belt.

"If you could just *think*," Jessica pleaded. "You may have information that you don't think is very important but it could be *vital*."

Pengelly kept on shovelling.

Jessica sighed.

All this trouble for a pair of old shoes, she thought. *Here I am in a leaky cave; I've been flung around like a yo-yo until I was sick, I've fallen through a hole, I've probably broken something, I haven't had any muncheon and Miss Strega has disappeared. I might just get on my broomstick and fly home.*

Berkeley, perched on her shoulder, gave her cheek an encouraging pat with a feathery wing.

Jessica tried again.

"A very *famous* Oracle thinks that you can solve this mystery."

"I told you I know nothing about any Dame's shoes. Now clear off."

"Ha-ha!" Jessica said, shining the Lantern Fish on Pengelly's face. "I didn't say anything about a Dame."

"You didn't?"

Pengelly shuffled backwards out of the light.

Jessica followed him.

"Tell me what you know!" she demanded, sounding much braver than she felt.

"Why should I? What's in it for me?" demanded Pengelly, belligerently.

Jessica waved the Lantern Fish in his face. "I could turn you into a bat or a slow worm. I'm good at transforming, I am, with or without a wand."

"Oh for crying out loud!" the gnome shrieked. "I'll tell you everything; just turn off that light."

Chapter Six

"You'd better come this way."

Pengelly, grumbling, led Jessica down the stone staircase. He let her keep the Lantern Fish pin on as long as she just shone it on her feet to see where she was going. Water dripped down the walls and plip-plopped on to the steps.

"We don't go out much, us gnomes," he told her. "I don't like daylight, and moonlight is not much better. I like being underground, doing my work, mining gold like my dad and his dad before that. But Mugwump—" Pengelly stopped suddenly and jabbed his index finger at the side of his head, "Mugwump is different. She likes to go Up There. She's not a garden gnome, don't get me wrong, she's not that bad. But she keeps old stuff..." He lowered his voice. "She has a *hoard*."

"A hoard?" Jessica repeated, excited. "And you think she has Dame Walpurga's shoes?"

Pengelly snorted. "I'm only saying..." He rummaged in his pocket and pulled out a crumpled piece of paper, "…that I found this on the floor a week ago."

Jessica shone the light of the Lantern Fish torch on it and read:

The Dress Shoes worn by Dame Walpurga of the Blessed Warts at the Signing of the Treaty to End the Broomstick Battles.

"That's amazing! I've seen this before. It's the sign from the Feet First Fund museum. Tell me at once where to find this Mugwump."

"This is as far as I go," declared Pengelly, stopping at the foot of the staircase. "You're on your own from here on."

He hoiked across a dingy ragged curtain. "Behold Mugwump's lair."

And with that, he turned on his feet and

scuttled back towards his mine, sniggering unpleasantly.

Jessica moved her torch from left to right and right to left and up and down.

If this was a *hoard*, it was a far cry from what she had been expecting. Where were the gold goblets? The silver swords? The chests of antique coins?

Ahead of her, for as far as she could see, there were towering heaps of black plastic bin liners jumbled up with stacks of newspapers, broken bicycles, tangles of headphones, balding cuddly toys and pyramids of old clothes. There were crates of empty bottles, a mound of out-of-date computers, a baby grand piano without a lid, several sofas spilling yellow foam and a baby's buggy with a twisted wheel. She turned back to give Pengelly a piece of her mind for wasting her

time when she heard the heavy tramp tramp of a pair of hob-nailed boots approaching and the sound of a female voice singing.

"I'm a second-hand gnome in my second-hand home..."

The music stopped. Jessica heard a loud sniff.

"I do believe I smell a visitor."

Jessica moved swiftly behind the dingy old curtain as Mugwump trundled into view. She was like Pengelly, short and round with a pointy head and a pair of thick glass-bottomed spectacles, except that she didn't have a beard and instead of scowling like Pengelly, she looked radiant. She beamed. She leapt up onto a pile of plastic bin bags and hopped over them like a mountain goat.

"Come on," she said cheerfully, "I know you're here somewhere. Stop messing about! You can't fool Auntie Mugwump!"

Jessica peered around the curtain.

Mugwump looked as harmless as she sounded but, after the night she had had, Jessica wasn't taking any chances. She stayed behind the curtain and called out.

"Madam – I mean Auntie – Mugwump. Excuse me for intruding on your lair but my name is Jessica and I am on a very important quest on behalf of Witches World Wide. My bird, Berkeley, is going to fly over to you with a photograph of a pair of shoes.

Please look at it carefully and tell me if you have them."

She put the photograph in Berkeley's beak and sent her off.

"My, oh my," said Mugwump. "What an unexpected pleasure! A witch and her mascot! If I'd known you were coming, I would've baked a cake."

She graciously accepted the photo from Berkeley's outstretched beak. "Oh yes, I have these. And what a lovely pair of shoes they are. Just look at the quality of that tassel. I think you'll find that is pure Italian silk. And those pearl buttons. I'd bet my bottom dollar that they are real oyster pearls."

Jessica was so annoyed that she flew out

from behind the curtain and landed a bit lopsidedly on the junk heap beside Mugwump.

"But they don't belong to you. They are *historic*! They are a *relic*! They're no good to *anyone* but the Feet First Fund."

Mugwump looked crestfallen. "But I found them."

"You stole them!" Jessica corrected her.

Now Mugwump looked indignant. "That is a monstrous lie! I found them in a wheelie bin round the back of Coven Garden. Wait!"

She bent down and began to rummage among her plastic bags. "Here they are! I will not have my good name smeared. You can have them!"

And she thrust the bag with the shoes into Jessica's hands.

Jessica looked at the bag.

Was that it? Was her quest over, just like

that? And what was all that about a wheelie
bin?

"I don't understand how or why you got
these, Madam – I mean Auntie – Mugwump,
but thank you for giving them back," Jessica
said. "Witches World Wide will be over the
moon. Berkeley and I will return the shoes to
Coven Garden right away."

"Not so fast, young lady!" came a voice
from the shadows. "I'll have those!"

Chapter Seven

Jessica and Mugwump nearly jumped out of their shoes with fright.

"Who's that?" they shouted.

"Just put the shoes on the ground and

move back behind the curtain and no one will get hurt," said the voice.

Mugwump and Jessica froze.

"Just do it!" snarled the voice. "And don't even think about drawing your wand!"

Jessica and Mugwump backed away.

As soon as they were behind the curtain, Jessica put a finger to her lips to warn Mugwump not to say a word.

Then she switched on her super-duper de-luxe invisibility-when-you-need-it cape and glided silently forward on her broomstick to see who would come out from the shadows.

For a couple of minutes, nothing stirred. Then there was a movement from behind one of the stone pillars and out scuttled a caped figure who moved swiftly towards the bag containing Dame Walpurga's shoes.

Jessica flew silently over her head as she bent down to pick it up.

"Gotcha!" Jessica pounced and grabbed the back of the mysterious figure's cape.

"You fool! You can't stop me," the witch shouted. Even though she couldn't see Jessica, she managed to seize her ear and pull on it very hard.

"Ouch!" shouted Jessica, jabbing her with an elbow.

The two of them fell back, grunting. They rolled over and over Mugwump's stacks of newspapers, upsetting bottles, plinkity-plonking over the keys of the grand piano and collapsing on to a broken sofa as both struggled to hold on to the shoes.

White smoke began to pour from the witch's nostrils and her features began to dissolve.

"Ah-ha!" Jessica muttered, "You won't catch me out with the old witch-switch trick."

So when the witch turned into a pillar of smoke, which made Jessica want to sneeze, she clung on to her end of the bag.

When the witch changed into a stream of fast-flowing water, which froze Jessica's fingers to the bone, she didn't unclench her fists.

When the witch became a fluttery bird, which flickered its wings and tickled Jessica's chin, she never let go.

Behind them Mugwump oohed and aahed and leapt around, rescuing falling stacks of papers and tripping over trailing computer wires.

"By the raucous squawking of the peacock," shouted the mystery witch, returning to her everyday shape. "Enough of this! Let's see who you are."

Jessica undid the invisibility clasp of her cape with one hand but still held firmly onto the stumpy heels of Dame Walpurga's shoes with the other. She stared indignantly at the other witch. "I'm Jessica, witch-in-training. Who are you?" she demanded.

"I am Professor Cobbleroni, the Head Finder and Seeker…"

Jessica gasped. "…of the Fancy Footwear Foundation… Heckitty Darling's rival!"

"Yes, and I stake our claim to these shoes. I knew they were in Walpurga's well, whatever Heckitty Weckitty says. I had just gone to get a fishing line and when I came back, she had fished them out herself."

Oh my, thought Jessica. *Could that be true?* "But you stole them back!" she said. "I just took them for safekeeping," Professor Cobbleroni said with a careless wave of her hand, which gave Jessica the chance to take the bag with the shoes.

"I hid them in the wheelie bin and went off to tell President Shar Pintake my side of the story, but before I had a chance, someone had raised the alarm and got up a witch hunt. Then when I went back to the bin, the shoes were... gone!" Professor Cobbleroni's voice trembled just as Heckitty Darling's had.

Jessica passed her a handkerchief and while Professor Cobbleroni dabbed her nose, enquired, "So tell me, what does the Fancy Footwear Foundation have in its collection?"

Professor Cobbleroni cheered up. "Oh lots! We have the Sleeping Beauty's wedding shoes and one of Cinderella's glass slippers. We have a pair of charred bootees that belonged to the witch who made the Gingerbread House. She was one of the last old-fashioned witches, you know, the kind with iron teeth who liked to eat children for breakfast. And, as luck would have it, after I heard about your quest and decided to follow you, I found a fabulous pair of giant's seven league boots lying out there on the mountainside."

Jessica tapped the side of her nose. "They belong to Don Gigantesco actually and he'll probably come after them – he's not the kind of giant who gives presents to witches. But seriously, Professor, I have an idea that could make everybody happy."

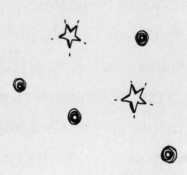

Chapter Eight

Two columns of witches in their best capes, hats, stripy stockings and shiny footwear stretched all the way along Coven Garden Avenue when Jessica and Miss Strega flew

there the very next evening. President Shar Pintake, in her ceremonial jade and purple sash, was standing at the great arched door beneath a huge banner.

Grand Opening
The fancy feet first
footwear fund foundation

On the President's left stood Heckitty Darling, bearing a large black satin pillow.

On her right stood Professor Cobbleroni, bearing another large black satin pillow.

Jessica carefully placed one of Dame Walpurga's lost and found shoes on each of them.

Heckitty and the Professor, still carrying Dame Walpurga's shoes on the black satin pillows in one hand, immediately seized Jessica by the elbows. They steered her up the grand staircase at such a cracking pace that her feet hardly touched the ground.

Jessica looked back over her shoulder to see if Miss Strega was following but her teacher had been swallowed up in the sea of witches flowing up the stairs.

They ushered her past the legendary Old Woman's Shoe (she had so many children she didn't know what to do) and into a room as long as a ballroom, as high as a cathedral and stuffed from floor to ceiling with shoes – nothing but shoes.

"These," said Heckitty, pulling her off to

the right, "are the bootees that belonged to the Wicked Witch of the West."

"But these," countered Professor Cobbleroni, pulling her by the left elbow, "are the red shoes that belonged to the Wicked Witch of the East: the very ones that Dorothy wore when she went to see the Wizard of Oz."

Heckitty yanked her away. "But these

dinky red shoes were made by the Shoemaker for the Helpful Elves."

Professor Cobbleroni picked up a long pointy metal shoe with ferocious spurs. "St George was wearing this when he slew the dragon. He gave it to me himself."

Heckitty threw her eyes up to heaven and steered Jessica towards a beautiful pair of jewelled sandals with toes that curled up at the ends. "These belonged to Scheherazade, the storyteller and enchantress of the 1001 Arabian Nights! Beat that, Cobbleroni!"

"That's enough!" Shar Pintake roared. "We're all in this Fancy Feet First Footwear Fund Foundation together."

Heckitty and Professor Cobbleroni backed away from the president's flying spittle.

"Now, Jessica, if you please."

Jessica made a deep bow and presented

her with the matching pillows with Dame Walpurga's lost and found dress shoes.

All the witches cheered and stamped their feet and waved their brooms above their heads until Shar Pintake silenced them by holding up her silver mace.

"Today," she said, "is a day of great joy when we honour Jessica Diamond as a Full Witch in recognition of her services to witchery. Not only has she returned Dame Walpurga's lost shoes but she has put an end to the rivalry between the Feet First Fund and the Fancy Footwear Foundation." Shar Pintake paused to stare meaningfully at Heckitty Darling and Professor Cobbleroni. "For the first time in history, Cinderella's glass slippers are re-united and the Bootees of the Wicked Witch of the West and the red shoes of the Wicked Witch of the East are under the same roof. Oh happy day!

Jessica, will you please step forward to accept this cauldron as a token of our gratitude?"

Jessica looked down at the audience, at all the smiling faces.

There was Dr Krank who had taught her how to make the General Purpose This-Will-Fix-It brew.

And Miss Wigg from the Coven Garden Theatre, who had given her her invisibility cape.

And Pelagia, the ex-pirate from the lighthouse on the Charm Archipelago, who had given her the Lantern Fish.

And there, waving enthusiastically and beaming from ear to ear, was her special guest – Auntie Mugwump.

But where on earth was Miss Strega? Tonight of all nights.

Jessica bowed in all directions as she accepted her new cauldron. "I am over the moon. I am thrilled to bits."

As the witches applauded and camera lights flashed and corks of special brew popped, Jessica struggled to make her voice heard. "I want to say a special thank you to someone without whom I would never have become a Full Witch."

Out of the corner of her eye, she could see Heckitty Darling and Professor Cobbleroni bickering again.

"And that person," Jessica was almost shouting, "is Miss Strega, the best witch trainer ever!"

Sadly, her words were drowned out in the general hugger-mugger.

Then people were thrusting microphones in her face.

"Jessica, what are your plans now that you are a Full Witch? Will you start your own business? What about Hollywood?"

"I'm not... I haven't... I won't...."

As soon as she managed to escape,

Jessica rushed to the library and ran right around the bookcases from Alchemy to Zymurgy, but Miss Strega was not there.

She slid down the banisters to the hall, ran across the spider-web floor and out on to the front steps where she looked up into the starry night sky. There was not a single broom rider to be seen, least of all Miss Strega.

"Oh where, oh where, can she be?"

Back she flew across the hall, past the portraits of famous witches and under the low doorway that led out to the Dame Walpurga Memorial Garden and Well (which as everybody knows is one of the Wonders of the Witch World).

The garden was deserted. Not a single witch was drawing up a bucket of magic water from Dame Walpurga's well. No one was queueing at the statue of Dame Walpurga to pat the wart at the end of her nose for good luck. Walpurga's magic hawthorn tree, adorned with all the little offerings of tiny broomsticks and scraps of cape, cast a long shadow across the lawn.

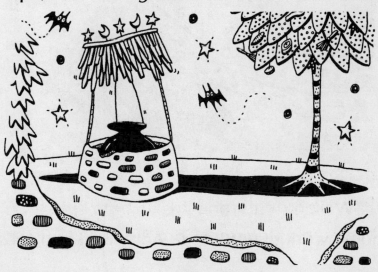

Jessica sniffed.

From behind the well, there came a familiar answering mew and out strolled Felicity – and Miss Strega!

"Oh, Miss Strega," Jessica cried, wrapping her arms around her, "I thought you had gone home without me!"

"Winking cats and frisky bats, Jess! Go home without you! As if. Actually, I had sort of hoped... well, Felicity and I have been talking things over... we were wondering... of course it mightn't be your cup of brew... now that you're a Full Witch... if you and Berkeley..."

"Blithering batwings, Miss Strega, of course I'd love to work with you!"

Miss Strega's long chin wobbled so hard you might have thought she was going to cry.

"Hu-eet," whistled Berkeley.

"Meeeooww," purred Felicity and she did a figure-of-eight around Jessica's legs.

Jessica slung her new cauldron on to the back of her broomstick. "Come on, team," she said. "Let's take to the air. We'll have a moon-vault and treat ourselves to the best muncheon ever. I'll brew."

Storyteller's Note

If, some day, you happen to be on the High Street, have a look for the shop where Jessica did her witch training. It's tucked in between the estate agents and the toy shop. The window display is as untidy as ever, with balls of twine, hurricane lamps, mouse traps and black cooking pots all in a jumble. But the creaking old shop sign has gone. There's a new one now.

Bella Strega & Jessica
Witch Suppliers

Spells to Order
No Quest too small

Printed by RR Donnelley at Glasgow, UK